Nick Smith was born in Bristol, England. His books include *Undead on Arrival*, *Milk Treading* and *The Kitty Killer Cult*. He lives on the panhandle of Northwest Florida.

Eat Happy

A stew of stories, poems & recipes

written & illustrated by Nick Smith

Also by Nick Smith

Fiction

Milk Treading
The Kitty Killer Cult
The Secret Life of Teddy Bears
Undead on Arrival

Non-Fiction

Fletcher Crossman: The Age of Endarkenment
Scriptwriting: The Secrets Unleashed

EAT HAPPY
A Stew of Stories, Poems & Recipes

Second US Edition

Recipes tested in the kitchen of
Dana Birlingmair

Author photograph by Dana Birlingmair

Library of Congress Control Number: 2018901415

ISBN-10: 0982889607
ISBN-13: 978-0982889602

A FIERCE Book
2707 Willow Grove Lane
Fort Walton Beach FL 32547

A version of "Sea Goat" was published in *Green Shoots #9*

"Night Tour" was previously published in *Book Banter*

"December Duet" was performed by Bob Sessions in the short film of the same name, directed by John Hood

Ingredients

Eat Happy

stories, poems and recipes

Nick Smith

He Must Still Earn Your Trust

Take one man with no heart
Nurture love for him until he grows the fragile sort
Suffer great pain as he takes too long to realize
That this heart is for loving.

Discard him for a while so he can feel
What you felt when he mistreated you
Accept him back as a full, honest man
Enjoy the spicy nights ahead.

Nick Smith

Eat Happy

As soon as I took a bite of my Eat Happy burger I knew something was wrong. But I didn't stop my meal.

This was a half pounder produced by the mightiest corporation in America, its billboards and logos brightening every skyline, urging me to enter their fast food joints and eat happy. Gobble up enough of these things, their ads told me, and mu urban ennui would vanish. I would be ecstatic and well fed. My entire world would become a circus of prankish joy, the Eat Happy mascot entertaining me whenever I got bored. So I ate the burger, even though this one tasted different.

It wasn't until I left the restaurant that my stomach began to hurt. I was used to burgers sitting in my stomach for a few hours as my body struggled to cram the cow in my colon. But now I felt a strange new sensation. As I walked down the high street the food seemed to move inside me, as if it was protesting its digestion.

I slumped against a store window, clutching my sizeable belly. I couldn't stand this thing writhing inside me. I crammed a finger down my throat, trying to make myself vomit. All that came up was bile and sauce.

I needed help, fast. I dragged myself back to the restaurant and hammered on the window. A guy dressed in a clown suit ran out and starting yelling at me, worried that I'd break the glass. That was the least of my concerns.

Bozo stood and gawped as blood seeped through my T-shirt. I lifted my shirt and saw an angry, crawling mess of meat and bun escaping from my belly button.

Nick Smith

The clown reached out a hand to try to stem the flow of blood, but he wasn't fast enough. My ribs collapsed onto my waist, no longer supported by my abdomen. Within minutes there was a hole where my torso used to be.

Through the window I saw customers writhing on the floor, food exploding from their stomachs in a shower of blood and pickles. Maybe some alien organism had infected the meat we were eating, or perhaps the burgers had just got sick of being chewed on and turned the tables. I wouldn't live long enough to find out. I used a familiar mantra to try to soothe myself in my last moments of consciousness. Small comfort, but better than none at all.

'Eat happy… Eat happy… Eat happy…'

Sea Goat

Breadcrumb chin and a voice of beer
Walking stick like a Zulu spear
Living under old tin roof
None save him can tell the truth

Salty tales of derring-do
Watch the patience wearing through
Sagas on the lowest seas
Misses grandkids on his knees

Can't remember food he's had
Or the first name of his dad
All his knowledge lost in time
Now the sea goat's past his prime.

Goat eyes fixed on blue front door
Only thing he's living for
Is to see some guests arrive
Queen bee daughter with her hive.

Kiddies bounce upon his lap
Queen bee shows her holiday snaps
But all that he can see
Is the bottom of the deep blue sea

On her second husband now
Daughter is a sacred cow
Beautiful in shanty song
Father's idol does no wrong.

Nick Smith

He tells of wartime ballyhoo
Long before his job fell through
Mermaid tails he's never seen
Chased by sharks and submarines

Stories that the world forgot
Swordfish nose heaved up with snot
Grabbed a Nazi by the throat
Victim of the savage goat

In the middle of his rant
Demonstrates on potted plant
German frogman is his prey
Spilled soil on the underlay
Proves how quick he doomed his foe
Drops the plant pot on his toe.

Queen bee buzzes round him fast
Teatime visits never last
He waves bye with naval cap
Settles down to have a nap

Nothing can be more envied
Than a soft pillow of memory
 Where all that you can see
Is the bottom of the deep blue sea.

Nick Smith

Tree Language

There was once a king who had a tall, beautiful tree in his royal garden.

The tree looked suitably majestic with its slender trunk, elegant branches and legions of shining green leaves. Courtiers would often visit the garden and lauded the king's fine horticultural judgment. They swore that on the calmest nights, they could hear the tree softly singing the praises of its master.

To ensure that it would never disgrace the palace by denuding itself, the king commanded that the tree should never shed its foliage. Afraid to disobey a direct ruling from its sovereign, it held onto its leaves with all its might.

When fall came the tree clenched its twigs and refused to let the leaves drop. They still turned brown, dead as dust. The tree forced all its sap into the leaves in a desperate attempt to revive them but it was too late.

When the king saw the tree in its withered, sorry state he ordered it chopped into firewood for the royal grate. The tree breathed a sigh of contentment. It had not broken its lord's commandment, and it would continue to serve him on his hearth.

The firewood lasted for a while, but the tree's sigh lasted much longer. If you listen closely you can still hear it in a forest breeze late on an autumn afternoon.

Nick Smith

Alien Babe

Last night you were in my dream
You'd snuck in through my window,
                           silent as a mouthless Grey
You stared at me with large dark eyes
Sizing up a man in black pajamas.

I couldn't move
Every muscle tensed up by your high tech ray
Your scary-long fingers brushed against my chest
Implanting your love in my heart

You left me blanked and bruised
Sore from your mischievous probes
The taste of space dust lingering in my mouth
Unsure of what was real

You left a scar
When you performed an autopsy on my soul
But I yearn for more of the same dream
You were the best two hours I ever lost.

Nick Smith

Egg Foo Yum

An Eat Happy recipe

INGREDIENTS

1 3 oz. pack Ramen noodles
1 egg
2 cups of water
Cheddar cheese to taste
2 slices of bread
Butter to taste

INSTRUCTIONS

Cook Ramen Noodles in a saucepan
Add the egg
Heat
Add seasoning
Add grated cheese, somewhat like a mouse
Scramble
Serve with bread and butter

Nick Smith

Sleeping Woman

I love your bunions
The way they glow when they've been angered
I love your eyes
Shot with blood and matched with bags
I love your hourglass ass
The hairs that rope round bars of soap
Your cellulite
Soft-patterned marble.

Your varicose veins
More intricate than a Roman mural
Your cauliflower ear
You cock to listen to me clear
Your clipped toenails
Snug beside me in my bed

Dandruff drops
Alighting on the curlers on your head
Your ashtray smile
That nicotine hit when you kiss me full on
Yellowed thumbs
Remain when all the smoke has gone

You're there for me
In full fat form I dream about your looks
Much more of you
Than the slim young things in modern books

Nick Smith

I'd miss your smell
That stale sweat that wakens me each day
Larger than life
Thank God your love is just a touch away.

Nick Smith

Hot and Bubbly

An Eat Happy recipe

INGREDIENTS

1 2 lb. bag of frozen hash browns
1 10½ oz. can of Cream of Chicken soup
2 cups of shredded sharp cheddar cheese
1 stick of butter
1 16 oz. tub of sour cream
4 rashers of bacon

INSTRUCTIONS

Thaw the hash browns
Place in a bowl with all except bacon
Mix well
Place in buttered 9x13" baking dish
Cook bacon
Crumble bacon
Sprinkle bacon onto the dish
Heat for 1 hour at 350°
Serve hot and bubbly

Nick Smith

Cold Feet

Warm petals drifting down
Escaping from the sun
Smothering me with fragrance
I drink in their sight

They cover the sidewalk
Transform its slabs into a bridal path
Daring me to tread
On their delicate remains

The tidy tree that loses them
Is nature's modest altar
Framed in thin green veils
Waiting for once-a-year worshipers

For once, its blossom shower
Cries for attention
Appreciating praise
As it bares all.

I leave the altar's shade
Skirt the petals, leave them lying
For other, braver souls
To crush beneath their feet.

Nick Smith

Light Sucks

Nick Smith

Prince Of The Playground

Lame ducks, that's what my mum calls my friends. She says I attract them like a magnet – uglies, dafties, orphans and weeds. I don't think they're lame, they just happen to be mates.

There's Nick Reilly with his thick spectacles and barking laugh, Mark Smythe who carries a briefcase everywhere and Richard Porter whose farts can kill a cat. They all think that Wayne Ting is weird.

The best thing about my block of flats in Lincoln, England is the park nearby. It has a football pitch and a lake and everything. When I was little my mum would always take me to feed the birds there. I'm too old for that now. When the ducks talk, it sounds like laughing to me – loud and harsh.

The first time I see Wayne he's making the ducks chuckle, got a good crowd going, throwing them generous chunks of bread. I can never eat crusts myself, or enders. They hurt my teeth.

I say hi to this loaf-chucking comedian and as he turns to look at me I get a surprise. I've never seen a Japanese kid before, not in real life anyway. The water behind him ripples in the wind. We don't have a conversation; we just look at each other, but the next day in school I feel like I know him when he walks in through the gates.

I go to Mill Crest School. It's a big red building, quite new, and across the busy main road there's a newsagent's and a launderette. Further along is a basketball court and the ruin of an old church, built 700 years ago, which Mrs. Kalmer makes us write about all the time.

She's a genuine menace, put on this earth to stop us having fun. She stands in the playground most breaks with her arms folded, a sour look on her face. She seems to have some kind of rascal radar, always knows when you're up to no good. When she catches you she comes down on you like a ton of bricks.

Nick Smith

The teachers think I'm a bit slow or stupid but I know I've got a lazy eye. Mum and Dad won't believe me even though I've got proof. Sometimes I hold my hand over the right side of my face and I can see the board better. I get very tired, especially on Friday afternoons when the time really starts to drag, daydreaming the last classes of the week away.

I can go for days without answering a question or even saying a word. Nick Reilly says I'm like a mime artist or a Thunderbirds puppet with no strings attached, just bobbing around. I don't laugh at his lame jokes. I ignore them, mind my own business. I always believe that if you don't rise to a bait, the barbs won't hurt. They do, though, and the jibes never stop so I isolate myself. I like it that way.

Everybody at Mill Crest wears a red jumper and carries a red book bag. You could have a great bullfight in our playground, with its walls as high as full-grown oaks. I'm the first person in the whole place to talk to Wayne – the lollipop lady doesn't count. I ask him where he's from and he says Tokyo. I wonder out loud if he's ever seen Godzilla and he smiles. Maybe that's why he's emigrated, because his city keeps getting squashed flat by giant monsters.

According to him, his dad is helping out at RAF Waddington. Wayne wants to be an airplane mechanic too, but he has to survive our school dinners first.

The new boy turns out to be much sharper and brighter than me so I sit next to him in class to copy his work. It's a lot easier to see a piece of paper on the desk beside you than it is to look at the board across the room. Wayne doesn't mind me bugging him – he probably likes the company. I remember how lonely I felt when I started at Mill Crest.

At break time I ask Wayne more about his family. All I know about Japan comes from games and cartoons, but everybody's got relatives. He tells me that his mum is a lawyer, his sister is ancient (thirty-one) and his granddad is in America.

'He was held prisoner during the Second World War,' says Wayne quietly. 'After Pearl Harbor was attacked. For four years they didn't trust him, then when the fighting stopped they set him free and he went back to work.'

All my Gramps ever does is build computers that blow up when you try to use them. I wish I had a family as exciting as Wayne's.

Nobody can go to our school without getting picked on by Billy Fleming. Billy's from Falkirk, a rough Scottish town where you have to grow up fast, so he's more mature than most of the kids in our year. Wayne's been warned to stay away from the bully but he can't shake him; it's as if Billy's taken a shine to him. They're both from out of town, exotic for a small city like Lincoln, so there's no excuse for them to start fighting.

It starts with the names. *Slant eyed rice eating yellow nip.* That's a bit much, considering natural born Lincolners are also known as Yellowbellies. Billy's testing the new kid, trying to needle him, waiting for a response. In my experience the victims either run off crying or get angry and raise their fists. Wayne does neither.

A crowd of Year Fours huddle round the out-of-towners, yelling and giggling. *Fight fight scrap!* Their raucous laughter reminds me of those hungry ducks. There's nothing more guaranteed to bring a teacher running but before the crowd scatters Billy gets one good punch in, knocking Wayne onto his back. There's a nasty crack as his head hits the ground.

I know exactly how the new kid's feeling, I've been there myself. Completely alone, no safety, no mummy or daddy to help you. Cold and ashamed, trying to be brave.

Mrs. Kalmer breaks things up right enough, parting the red-jerseyed sea, her loudhailer lungs petrifying everyone in the yard. She offers to help Wayne onto his feet but he gets up on his own, rubbing his sore skull; he knows how important it is to look independent. Another show of weakness now and he's dead.

Nick Smith

'Why?' he asks me, already knowing the answer. If Wayne wasn't Japanese he'd be picked on for another reason – wearing the wrong shoes, being too clever, supporting Notts Forest.

'I need some help with my homework,' I tell him, staring at the bruise round his eye. He'll have a shiner in the morning – I wonder if he'll have sight problems like me? He nods and offers to write it up for me and he's as good as his word.

Next morning I pile through a throng of skittish schoolkids searching for my little helper. He's squatting in a corner of the yard and I assume he's playing Beyblade. Japan's where all that stuff comes from, the toys and the trading cards, so it's natural that he'll be a class act player. Instead he digs a small leather bag from his pocket and dips a dirty finger inside. A few younger kids watch, mucho curious.

He selects a glass ball from the pouch and holds it up to his black eye. I don't know where marbles come from; I wouldn't have guessed Tokyo. Anyway, this is like no marble I've seen in all my puff. It holds loads of different patterns, all the colors of the rainbow helter skeltered together. As the sun glints off the sphere I catch my breath. It's beautiful.

Wayne draws a circle on the ground with a mucky piece of bark. He pours his bag of marbles into the circle and invites the little kids to play a quick pre-registration game. Using the helter skelter marble he flicks the other balls out of the circle in quick succession, an "amazing display of skill" as the TV commentators say.

I sidle up and ask him if he's got any lunch money to share with me. He says no because his dinner's all paid for. I stand there and watch instead, enjoying the game and the sunshine.

It can take less than a week for a craze to sweep our school and the marble thing is no exception. Within a few days everybody's into it (including me) and the local shops are sold out. Wayne has gone from victim to victorious with one flick of his fingers.

Eat Happy

I don't usually remember my dreams but something starts to stick – the image of that special marble. Wayne's brought all kinds with him, reflective silver and gold ones, large and small, clear and misty. He even has one that looks like a bloodshot eyeball, which is great fun to watch roll around the yard. Mrs. Kalmer shrieks and jumps five feet in the air when she sees it! But the one that caught my eye seems unique. I want it.

In science Mr. Dolkins closes the blinds and switches off the lights for a video. It's something about smoking and we're all bored within seconds; our science teacher is famous throughout the East Midlands for being deadly dull. When Wayne looks half-asleep I take my chance, borrow his leather pouch and peer inside. Even with my poor vision that helter skelter belter stands out. I remove it, breathless, expecting Wayne to wake up or the teacher to see me at any moment. I put it in my pocket and replace the pouch exactly where I found it.

The merchandise is too hot to use in the playground, even though I want to show it off to everybody. Instead I keep tabs on Wayne, waiting for him to notice what's missing. At lunchtime he takes out his pouch, ready for a game with a couple of fifth formers. He delves deep, fumbling for his pride and joy. When he realizes it's gone he doesn't get upset or angry; he looks sad, stands still for a short while, then selects another marble and gets on with his game. This doesn't exactly fill me with glee.

If Wayne isn't going to get all upset, why bother? I am the owner of a stolen glass ball that no one can see, at least not 'til the marble craze is over. Then what would be the point? I have to return the goods to their rightful place.

'Billy Fleming!' I turn, mouth open in a guilty O. Mrs. Kalmer doesn't look happy. She's got her arms folded as usual and the breeze has blown her hair into a wild mess. 'What's that you've got there?'

I obviously look shifty enough to arouse her suspicion and I can no more stop my cheeks glowing red than I can help myself as I open my right hand, palm upwards. There the rainbow marble glistens and I look down at it, unable to meet the teacher's glare.

Nick Smith

'I've had as much as I can stand of you, Billy Fleming. Come with me. You too, Wayne.' The new kid breaks off his game and follows us meekly to the head's office.

'I was borrowing it, wasn't I mate?' I ask Wayne, mentally urging him to confirm my high-rise story. He says nothing.

'Then why did you report it stolen, Wayne? Has this boy been bothering you?' I've already been suspended once for knocking one of Nick Reilly's teeth out – this could be the clincher.

Wayne looks disappointed but to his credit he does not grass me up. I can rely on my friends to keep schtum as they know what'll happen to them if they don't. As he stands before the headmaster, hands clasped in front of him, I remember what he told me about his granddad – picked on simply because he was Japanese. Although I wouldn't call myself a softhearted guy, I sympathize with him.

We escape from the office with a rap on the knuckles, and I vow to be kinder to Wayne in future. He gives me a wide berth. I see him now and again, Prince of the Playground, helping his schoolmates to improve their marbling skills.

It wasn't Wayne's possession I was jealous of, it was his rising popularity. Nobody wants to spend time with me – not unless I make them. Although I call Nick and Mark my friends, to them I'm a bully. Until Wayne arrived I was special, the Scottish boy with an interesting background and an unusual accent. Now I'm another lame duck, alone and ashamed, trying to be brave.

The Moon Is Bright Tonight

The moon is bright tonight.
The world is vast and ready to explore
Yet you choose to watch it through a tiny window
When I'm walking the dogs,
Our little wirehair and bigger collie-Dalmatian mutt.

I reach up a hand and feel
I can almost reach the powerlines that
      stretch over our street.
A span beyond are the stars,
Teasing with twinkles, promising a warm glow.

Even with a ten-foot ladder
I'd get up there into the night sky and find them cold and distant
An illusion I never stop reaching for.

Nick Smith

I Wouldn't Like To Meet Him In A Dark Alley

A Bad Crime Story

Doug felt nervous when the Detective Inspector Gore came to question him. He picked at his fingers, cleaned his fingernails and twiddled his thumbs.

'Tell us what you say,' said the cop in a pinstripe suit. Doug cleared his throat, playing for time enough to avoid the wrong thing to say at the right time.

'I don't know really. Is that an Armani?' Doug asked.

The man shook his head with a trace of a smile. 'JC Penney. I know this might be difficult for you, Mr. Jones. You're still in shock. Believe me, I know how you're feeling. Cops aren't immune to trauma and I've seen plenty of bloody messes in my time. I still wanna throw in my machine-sewn pocket. You can talk to me. This is your best chance to say your piece.'

Doug nodded and began his story.

'I was walking down Drove Loan, took a right, then a left, then another left. Passed an alleyway and stopped. I heard a cry, saw too guys squabbling. One of them was tall and thin, the other was short and fat. He had a knife.'

'Who did?'

'The short one. Little guy, big blade.'

As Doug talked, the cop in the suit wrote notes on a small pad.

'They were arguing about something, I don't know what. The tall boy pulled out a gun and he shot the man with a knife.'

'He shot the man… with a knife?' the cop sounded chary. 'What happened next, Mr. Jones?'

'I ran away.'

'I see.' The policeman stood up, strolled around the room. 'If you ran away,' he said suddenly, 'why were your fingerprints on the gun?'

Doug felt sweat run down his face. He thought he'd been careful, wiping the weapon clean with his handkerchief. He must have left some evidence after all.

'I was curious,' said Doug, 'went to see if I could help the dead man. But… he was dead.'

'Changing our statement, are we?'

'I guess.'

'That's all for now, Mr Jones. Thanks for your time etc.'

Detective Inspector Gore left Doug's apartment and made his way to his car. The walk took him through a dark alleyway, where Doug was waiting for him.

'I want to make one more change to my statement,' said the suspect, pulling a revolver from his sock. 'I killed a policeman as well.'

'When was that?'

'Now.' Doug killed a policeman and went home to eat some beans.

No Permanent Someone

You have no one to iron your shirts any more
No one to keep you warm every night
No one to tell you they love you every chance they get
No one to chop the ginger for your tea.

You have no one thinking of you every moment of every day
No one to share all your secret fears
No one bringing you coffee in bed
You have no permanent someone
But you get your own way.

Nick Smith

Blank Space Baby

Nick Smith

Caitlin's White Christmas

Annoyingly, the sun beat down on Lincoln, England again.

Caitlin Peek desperately wanted it to snow but the TV weatherman said it was too warm and dry; a white Christmas was out of the question. This wasn't good enough for the little girl with dense locks of dark hair, a bairn of great brain and resource who'd been waiting all winter for sledding and snowball fights.

'Mummy,' she asked, pulling at the hem of her long-suffering mother's blouse, 'how will Santa ride his sleigh across the rooftops if there's no ice to slide on?'

Caitlin's mum Becky sat at her computer working on her latest work-from home scheme. She was a veteran entrepreneuse. She'd tried reflexology, Reiki, sports massage, brain stem keyhole surgery, teaching the violin, making chocolate pilchard sandwiches to sell to the motorists jamming up the streets at rush hour; she'd given bathtime aquarobics instructing, internet auctioneering, bookbinding and taxidermy a try. But there was only so much room in the house for self-help manuals and Becky was torn between spending time with her daughter and going the self-employed route.

The boiler was on the blink again and Becky was glad of the warm spell. Yet she took pity on her daughter and said, 'the reindeer will probably find it easier to walk around if it isn't slippery. They'll be able to go faster, so that no children will miss out on getting their presents.'

'But I'll miss out!' Caitlin wailed. 'I WANT A SNOWMAN!'

Caitlin's parents had thought the three-foot high plush snowman from Homebase would sate her, but she wanted a real one with a carrot nose and ice castle eyebrows and everything. It was time for her dad, Ben, to take charge. Large in stature and spirit, he resembled Hollywood legend Adrian Brody with an arrogant crop of stubble and large puppy dog eyes. He took her ice-skating.

41

Nick Smith

The Saxilby Icekatorium was vast and dazzling, multi-colored ceiling lights hueing patrons in rainbow shades. Steam escaped from their mouths but they weren't cold; the skaters – young or infirm, rash or inexperienced – were dizzy with delight.

A blue-carpeted area led to the main counter, where Ben and Caitlin decided their boot sizes and a shaggy-whiskered youth handed them their footwear. Passing the pigeonholes full of hush puppies, trainers and Clark shoes, they reached the rink, a frozen reservoir of fun.

At first Caitlin didn't want to venture onto the rink, but as she watched the happy faces of the other skaters – especially the children – she bravely decided to give it a go.

Ben and Caitlin cut interesting figures as they stumbled onto the ice. At over six foot, Ben was the tallest person present. Once they'd got used to gliding on their blades and plucked up the courage to let go of the siderail, they did surprisingly well. Enjoying the sensation of movement___like floating along a conveyor belt___they relaxed and enjoyed themselves, ending with a Torville-and-Dean special, Ben lifting his daughter into his arms and carving a deft figure of eight in the centre of the rink. They didn't notice that all the other patrons had cleared off, fearing for life and limb; Ben and Caitlin were happy.

Still, in the time it took them to leave the rink, remove their skates and drive home, Caitlin returned to her favorite subject. Ben told her to change her tune, and that record was Bing's biggest hit.

'I NEED A WHITE CHRISTMAS!'

'There's a few days 'til Santa comes,' her dad said patiently, 'there may still be time for snow.'

Next morning when Ben had gone off to work Caitlin decided to take the matter into her own hands. She dragged a stepladder from the hallway into the living room, nicked her dad's powerdrill from the garage and used it to attack the white-stuccoed ceiling. All she succeeded in doing was to make a tiny hole. She drilled a few more then, realising that the noise was causing the cats to eat their feet, put the drill and the ladder away. Her mum, still hard at work in the back room, was listening to rave music on her headphones. She was pleased that her daughter was playing more quietly than usual.

Ben let himself into his neat, tastefully decorated home, whistling a cheeky tune. Caitlin was in the living room looking angelic as pie, playing her ladybird game.

'Daddy!' she cried. 'I want juice.' Becky came in to say hello. As Caitlin rushed to wrap her arms round her dad the ceiling gave way and the family were showered in white plaster.

'It's snowing!' Caitlin squealed.

Ben and Becky were understandably annoyed. Becky turned red. Ben put his hands on his ears to keep the steam in. Caitlin rolled a handful of the plaster flakes into a ball and lobbed it at her dad's belly. Her aim was a little low and like Queen Victoria, he was not amused.

'That does it!' Ben bellowed. 'I'm putting you in Barry's garden.' Caitlin's face fell – this was a fate worse than Detford. Barry's garden was full of runner beans and Caitlin hated vegetables with a green-fingered passion.

With the little girl tucked under his arm, Ben dragged her kicking and yipping out of the house. He was about to toss her over the hedge when something stopped him in his tracks… a cold drip onto his nose. Unearthly crystals floating onto his head. He lifted Caitlin into an upright position and they gazed at the sky together, amazed.

Within minutes, Becky and Ben had cooled down, Barry's garden didn't look so green and the whole world was turfed white.

'I guess you got your Christmas wish,' Ben murmured.

'What do you want Santa to bring you, Daddy?'

'An interior decorator. And a pair of ice skating boots for us all.'

Nick Smith

Bowtie Bonanza

An Eat Happy recipe

INGREDIENTS
1 x 1 lb. box of farfalle pasta
12 oz. of Italian sausage
1 x 28 oz. can of crushed tomatoes
1 x 10 oz. can of Rotel original diced tomatoes and green chilies
1 pint of half and half
2 tbs. olive oil
1 cup chopped onions
1 heaped tbs. flour
Parmesan cheese

INSTRUCTIONS
In a large saucepan, cook the onions in olive oil until they soften
Remove Italian sausage casings and crumble into the saucepan until browned (no pink)
Push sausage and onions into a corner
Pull drippings to other side
Add flour to drippings and mix well (no lumps)
Incorporate with sausage and onions
Pour in crushed tomatoes and Rotel
Cook on medium high heat for 15 minutes
Cook the pasta according to package directions
Reserve a third of a cup of pasta water, drain the rest
Add pasta water to sauce
Serve pasta in bowls
Top with sauce and Parmesan

Nick Smith

Jack

In my youth I was a bonfire
Burning on my birthday to keep evil spirits away
As years went on my fire dimmed
Sapped to a flickering pinprick candle light
Shining from a masked gourd
On stoops of men too ignorant to fear the night.

My pulpy innards disemboweled
I stink of singeing ugly flesh
Mouth all jagged, sharp eyes cowled
I sear the flies that seek to steal my breath.

Foolish children dress as ghouls
Beg for treats once used to please sad wraiths
Scamper on streets far darker than they know
Kept safe by my feisty little glow.

Don't let me rot away
An unlit husk's no help against hell's spawn
Kindle my amber lantern flame
I'll stand 'til Hallow's Eve is wan.

I see the figures in the shadows
Through my rough cut ruby eyes
And pray the demons of the night don't play a trick
For death can be the nastiest surprise.

Nick Smith

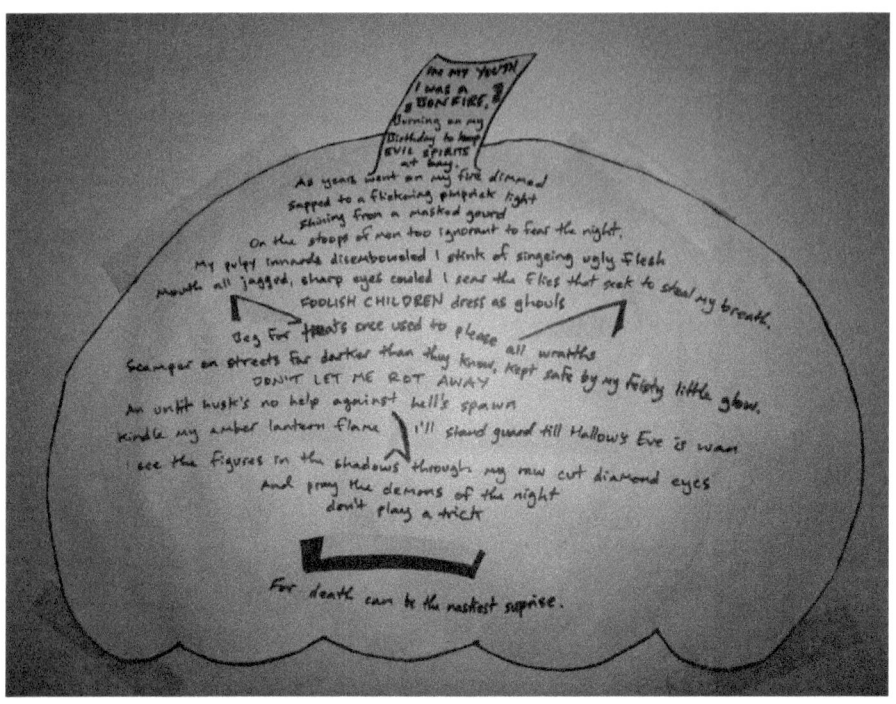

Night Tour

When the sun lays its healing rays on Edinburgh, the city warms and glows as if it's beaming. The flora of Princes Street gardens take on a lush hue; the columns that front the National Gallery resemble a row of smiling, pearly teeth. No matter how hard the wind blows, those columns maintain their skinny grin. They know that they guard a building filled with laughter and lies, the kind you can only hear when you take the night tour.

You won't find this tour in any of the brochures. Only the canniest of visitors know of it – perhaps a couple have taken a wrong step on a ghost walk, lost their way, found a trail that's altogether more magical and mysterious.

The night tour is a well-kept secret, known to locals who care to take an interest in their surroundings, never forgotten by visitors who stumble upon it. Your guide is a will-o'-the-wisp, an indigenous know-it-all who won't regale you with half-baked tales or tawdry gossip. He will lead, explain, and try to keep you out of trouble.

Start at the old Leith station, where trains shuggle by. If you're patient, one will take you up the Walk to the city center. Visit the castle at night and you'll see Robert the Bruce's Foot Soldiers resurrected to the constant drumming of a dark tattoo.

At the Writers' Museum, you'll find Robert Burns doodling at his desk, one hand clapping the faithful dog that sits at his feet. If you feel up to the task, you can challenge Sir Walter Scott to a game of chess, although the sound of his printing press can be distracting. It churns out the pages of The Bestiary, a lost Waverley novel, and it's worth sparing a glance at those unforgettable excerpts:

Nick Smith

What e'er the dusk-dimm'd clouds may hide
Stray moonlight through the wisps will slide
And show the way for those who try
To look for answers, question why
The wretch'd shadows dare to hide
The places with doors open wide
To let light out and warm their guests
Fickle enough to end their quests.

Stop at St. Giles Cathedral and you'll hear the future sounds of devout congregations, pledging devotion in a soulless world. You'll see the High Kirk's crown glitter and be captivated by the siren sound of a gargoyle's bagpipes.

If you have the time, nip over to Bruntsfield where the Royal Observatory is a must; just as the stars speak to us from the past with their restive gleam, so do the folks of the Old Town if the telescope's lenses are tilted towards the city streets.

Then go to the National Gallery, through those gritted teeth, and inhale the smell of an old woman cooking eggs. Here the Christ Child sleeps watched over by his mother, while across the way Reverend Robert Walker skates gracefully on Duddingston Loch. He's so elegant that he almost seems to be gliding on thin air.

Three Graces huddle together, trying to keep their marble flesh warm. The Ladies Waldegrave mirror the Graces' trinity, although they pointedly ignore the statues. The ladies prefer to hang out with the Honorable Mrs. Graham, who spends her days looking longingly at her companions, wishing she was having as much fun as them.

If you've brought the children along, they're sure to enjoy playing in Monet's haystacks or climbing the Montagne Sainte-Victoire. The Calvinist portraits won't approve, of course, but don't worry; they're too conformist to leave their frames. Parents concerned with the education of their children may choose to drop them off at the School of Apollo for a masterpiece masterclass.

On the night tour you can also take them to the Museum of Childhood on the High Street; all the display cases will be open and the lifelike prepubescent mannequins will invite you to play with their toys. Explore the deeps of the museum and you'll find a tiger that once growled and roared fiercely, stretching its back, yawning, reliving its glory days on safari, hunting for humans to stuff its belly.

So long as you stick close to your guide, this is just one of many highlights on a tour of echoes, reflections of things gone and things yet to come. It's a deeply held secret but keep your eyes open, listen carefully, and you'll find it. The trail is all around you.

Nick Smith

Ghost Cycle

Andy didn't like riding home from school on winter evenings. It got so dark so early that by the time the final bell rang the sky was dark. Though he'd lived in his little Michigan town all his life, he could never remember a time when all the streetlights worked. There were long patches of unlit road where Andy couldn't see the pavement. Since he'd been cycling to and from school all year, he knew where all the potholes were. He could swerve round all the cracks made by errant tree roots. He rode boldly over any other obstacles.

Andy had good Kevlar tires on an old Schwinn bike, the frame a little too high for his skinny young body. The saddle was uncomfortably hard. The spokes were rusty. The rubber was rotting off the handles. The spiked pedals, designed for long-distance riding, tore holes in his Skechers.

But it was *his* bike. He'd paid for it out of his lawn mowing earnings. He kept the tires inflated and the quick-release wheel locks tight; sometimes he even checked the brakes. None of his schoolmates had a classic like this and he felt if he pedaled fast enough he could go anywhere, far away from schoolwork and mom and dad and his annoying little sister Bonnie.

Tonight he was hungry. He headed straight home, bugs chirruping from the bushes as he whizzed by as if they were begging to hitch a ride, 'taxi! Taxi!' His short blonde hair ruffled in the cold night breeze – he refused to wear a helmet, that was for sissies – and he felt a chill through his uniform. The four mile ride would warm him up.

The heater was always cranked up in the school bus but Andy hated the yellow rotbox. The few times mom and dad had put him on it, it felt wrong. Too noisy. Too many bad smells, strange kids, clowns in their cliques, mean seat-hoggers, crybaby boys, girly girly gossiping girls, sports nuts, candy trolls, hall monitor wannabes, gamer goons, bug-eyed bullies, silent types, loners, moaners, perfect skin toners, Bieber bashers, forwardly fashionable fakers, sauerkraut-sick exchange students, math clones, earbud mutes, thumb-sucking fetal sleepers, silly band stalwarts, crammers, hungry Government lunchers, bleary-eyed bed heads and dark-clad chaos makers.

It was a big bus.

 Steering them all was Stoker, a crabby old man with fingers stained nicotine yellow. When Stoker swerved out of his lane, almost hitting a white van, Andy told mom. No more bus rides. He got to school on his own on his rickety Schwinn.

The school traffic far behind him, he took to the sidewalk to avoid a speeding motorist. The paving slabs were uneven, jolting him up out of his saddle. Uh oh. Andy's pale face shot right as he remembered the lush lawn outside the Golden Banquet Oriental Buffet. A green lawn meant sprinklers.

It was too late to stop or correct his path. Andy zoomed through an icy gauntlet of swamp –smelling water bursting over the lawn onto the sidewalk. How come he never avoided the sprinklers? Now he was cold, damp and close to a treacherous intersection.

The crossroads of Tingell and Partly was an accident that didn't have to wait to happen – collisions often did. There were three lanes on the school side of Partly was an accident, four wider lanes on Tingell and another turning lane onto Partly. Andy had to look five different ways to cut across. He had a couple of options: wait for a traffic light or hurtle across Tingell and hope he didn't get hit. He went for the crazy option. Switching his head from side to side, he pushed down hard on the pedals and gunned it across the main road.

Drivers liked to speed along Tingell, they liked to aim for cats shouting, 'die! Die!' but Andy wasn't a cat he was a daredevil stunt cyclist popping a wheelie to the finish line of the opposite sidewalk, laughing at the dumb joke in his head. Why did the chicken cross the road? He didn't. He was chicken.

Andy stopped on the other side of Tingell. No traffic. He'd been lucky again. He didn't wear earbuds, distracted by music on his bike – he always listened for oncoming cars. At that moment all he could hear was the thud of his heart, his quick short breaths. There was a car coming now, fast as his heart, headlights glaring with an angry blaze.

Another cyclist stood at the crossing, taller than Andy. As the headlights approached it was impossible for Andy to clearly make out the boy's features but he could see a black outfit and a spiked green helmet, a foot kicking down on a pedal, a motion forward.

'Stop! Don't!' Andy raised his hand, his mouth wide open as the rider tried to doge the approaching car. It was too close. He couldn't watch. He turned, heard shrieking brakes and a thud but no cry. Scared, Andy aimed his bike homeward and rode uphill. *That could have been me,* he thought. *Didn't that kid see the car coming?*

Despite a steep incline, Andy had to twitch his brakes as he passed a U-Haul depot. There was a side street there. He couldn't see if cars were coming so he prepared to stop if he had to. He glanced over his left shoulder to check for turning traffic, saw no vehicles on the road. There was no sign of an accident either. The other boy must have dodged the speeding car.

Relieved, Andy redoubled his speed and passed the hill crest, gaining momentum until he couldn't pedal anymore – gravity took over. He freewheeled over Muller Bridge then took a final uphill stretch, turning right onto the longest, darkest part of his journey – Fetch Road.

On his right was Mi Gente, the local Taqueria. Out back was a small restaurant with spicy food that smelled so good when it was being prepared in the mornings when Andy was on his way to school. On the way back the smells weren't so good: greasy garbage, rotting meat, thankfully layered under wafts of laundry detergent and softener. The rest of Fetch was so poorly lit that if Andy didn't keep heading in a straight line, he was liable to run off the road into one of the empty lots that made up its addresses.

Nick Smith

The road was creepy. A few cans had been left out for trash day, casting humanoid shadows in the vague moonlight. Andy peered ahead, tiring.

He heard a clicking sound behind him. He glanced over his shoulder and saw the older kid turn into Fetch. Relieved that the boy was okay, he raised a hand in acknowledgement. Took another look. Under his sick green helmet, the boy was horribly pale and his dark eyes stared right at Andy like a hunter's headbeams.

Maybe he doesn't want to run off the road either, Andy thought, praying for the moon to shine brighter and break the gloom around him.

Andy gripped his handlebars tight, clutching the grooves of cracked and broken rubber, focusing on the meager ray cast by his front bike light. He could hear the clicking of the strange boy's bike getting closer. Perhaps he was just taking the same route but the fearsome way he'd stared at Andy unsettled the schoolboy. Once he reached the corner he'd be close to home. That left turn onto Julian Road seemed so far away, though, and the road ahead was horribly dark.

Andy glimpsed a shadow out the corner of his eye. He wasn't sure if it was cast by his own lights or if his pursuer had closed in on him.

Don't turn around, he told himself. *Don't turn around. Duck your head down and keep pedaling. Get home. Get to safety, lock your doors, forget this happened.*

He couldn't help it. He looked back. There was nothing – no other bike, no pallid kid. He let out a deep breath. His imagination had got the better of him, fueled by the eerie night air. He was almost back at his house, out of the moonlight.

Finally he could see the turn for Julian, the street sign obscured by an errant oak tree. Five more minutes and he'd be in his kitchen foraging for an after-school snack. He allowed himself to freewheel for a moment. Heard the clack clack clacking sound again. Looked back.

The kid appeared out of the gloom right behind him, horrible face given a hellish hue by Andy's rear bike light. The devil kid stretched an arm out toward him, unnaturally long, clawing at his backpack.

Andy struggled to keep his balance and speed up. The kid had a good hold of his pack now and although he pedaled hard, Andy felt himself moving backward, a sensation like being tugged underwater into a bottomless inky sea.

With a scream he yanked his arms out of his pack, freed himself and turned onto Julian so fast he almost flew off the street. Straightening up he felt his heart racing, sight specked with light as it adjusted to the streetlamps ahead. He was alone, the creepshow kid left behind on Fetch Road. Andy had entered a residential area, one-story homes huddled close together, no place for a phantom.

Andy raced home and locked himself in his room. His folks weren't home from work yet. He dug a baseball bat from his closet and sat on his bed, knees up against his chest. He had no intention of going to look for his backpack – homework b damned. Tomorrow he would take the bus.

On his way to school on that noisy, crowded yellow beast, Andy didn't speak or share a seat with anyone. He kept looking out the window, afraid of what he might see.

The white cross surprised him. It was on the corner of Tingell and Partly; he'd never noticed it before. A shrine to a kid killed in a traffic accident, surrounded by flowers and old toys. Sitting on top was a green spiked bike helmet.

'Stop the bus!' Andy yelled, ignoring the derision of his fellow passengers as he jumped off to get a closer look at the shrine.

The cross was old, white paint flaking off the wood like snakeskin. The flowers had not been replenished for weeks and the whole shrine was layered with street dirt. At the base of the cross, a strip of card read:

Nick Smith

IN MEMORY OF BRENT MORROWS
1997-2013
DIED IN A HIT & RUN
WATCH THE ROAD

Watch the road. The words haunted Andy as he walked the rest of the way to school. On his way he saw a slew of lawns that needed to be mowed. It was time to save up for a car.

Fort Walton Beach, FL
October 21st 2014

Savage Tongue

When I was young
I didn't appreciate your savage tongue
Swallowing your bile
Was not my style.

But as time ticked
I learned to love your razor wit
And how your snide remarks
Always made the brightest sparks.

Now I volunteer
For you to chew my ear
Wittingly in the line of fire
To get hit by your belt-fed ire.

When you let loose
Feeling the need to cook my goose
I'll welcome that piece of your mind
It's love, of a kind.

Nick Smith

Nachos a Go-Go

An Eat Happy side dish

INGREDIENTS

1 lb. hamburger meat
1 16 oz. can of refried beans
2 cups of shredded Mexican cheese
1 8 oz. jar of taco sauce

Accompany with:
tortilla chips
sour cream
salsa
shredded lettuce

INSTRUCTIONS

Crumble and brown hamburger meat in saucepan
Drain the meaty juice
In a 9x13" baking dish, layer refried beans
Top with cooked hamburger, pressing down onto the beans
Pour taco sauce over the meat
Cover with shredded Mexican cheese
Bake for 20-30 minutes at 350 ° until the cheese is hot lava
Allow to cool for a few minutes
Serve with chips, salsa, shredded lettuce and sour cream. Dress it.
Undress it. Your choice

Nick Smith

The Serpent Was Right

You're in permanent trouble young lady. If you want to stumble into my house at this time of night drunk as a tequila worm, leaning against the dog for support, waking all the neighbors – the neighbors! What about your father and me? I'm not in the habit of running around in my undies, I'll have you know. Though it's a darn sight more than you wear to those clubs of yours.

We didn't have clubs in our day. We had our meeting places, where the young 'uns could get together, get to know each other better, canoodle up against an oak. We didn't wear skintight leathers or Britpop britches. We wore woolies and scarves, practical clothes. Our local cattle market was the pig farm.

We knew the boys would be there, slaughtering the swine in time for the Christmas rush. We would sit on the wall, our bums grey with mud, trying to attract their attention with fluttering eyelashes or a cry come-hither. They pretended to be involved in their work. We knew better.

The pigs floundered in the mud, wriggling from their executioners' clutches, spraying soil and worse in our direction. That made us giggle (the boys liked that). We had our personal favorites – mine was Brookie, a tall bloke with size 12 boots. It was his brother Brian who came after me, though. Maybe Brookie cared, maybe he didn't. I was too busy fending off his brother's advances to figure it out.

'I've got something for you,' said Brian, slithering towards me. I wanted to jump off my wall, go home but my friends were with me. They would have had to've gone home too. I had to be strong in front of them, put on an act. I told Brian to go away. He had bad acne, especially on his neck and chin. Like the scales of a snake.

His skin wasn't the only turn-off. There was something slithery about him that I didn't want to put my finger on, a primal red flag

63

waving in my mind. Still I was young and plain and I hadn't learned to read all the warning signs.

He persisted, one hand behind his back, clutching this great present of his. I rolled my eyes twice and asked him what it was. Pushing his hand gleefully at me, he showed me his gift. The head of a newborn piglet, brown and tattered at the ears.

'Get away from me you clodhopper!' I squealed, knocking the head out of my face. It rolled through the mud to the surviving pigs. They snuffled at it, not sure what it was. They still ate it though, hungry for that bloody stump head.

'I don't want to see you again,' I told Brian.

'You'll come back,' he replied. 'And you'll go out with me. Because you're lonely. I'll look after you and you'll look after me.'

And the serpent was right.

I did come back. I knew I couldn't be with Brookie, that I had to settle. And I was lonely, at least until I married Brian Worthing, abattoir artist.

So get up to bed now and no more of your noise, my bloody stump child, or your father'll take care of you. His swine-killing days are long gone but he's still the old snake he always was. Once he's got his fangs out you'll forget about your friends. Turn the light out on your way up and listen for his rattle.

Words Have Power

Don't ever upset or anger me
I'll destroy you with a few words
I won't say them to your face
I'll carve them on a slab, leave it for you to find

I know the power of words
Drunken, misspoken, never forgotten
I know the power of thoughts
Guarded under the breath

Your language sings inside
Like a scratchy pop hit
I tell you to change the record
Flip your tragic ballad of us

When you hit my needle nerve
With your soft sad tongue
I take Andy de los Santos' advice
And sing a silent Flintstones theme tune,
Praying to the Gods, Hanna and Barbera
To deliver me from your dastardly spite
Bedrock blocking our insane spats,
The limited animation of your fists.

When you make me sleep on the floor
Lying there, desperate to yabadabado you
My four-color dreams give me succor
Assured our soap will start anew at dawn.

Nick Smith

Curry is Life

An Eat Happy recipe

INGREDIENTS

1 4 oz. jar of Thai Kitchen red curry paste
2 x 131/2 oz. cans of coconut milk
2 boneless skinless chicken breasts
Veggies – handful each of cabbage, carrot, mushrooms, onions, flat snow peas
2 cups of cooked white rice

INSTRUCTIONS

Brown breasts on each side
Steam in a pan until tender
Shred chicken
Pour coconut milk and curry into the pan
Simmer to meld flavors for 12 minutes
Add chopped veggies, cook for 5 minutes
Serve on a bed of white rice

Nick Smith

The Hunter

It waited in the dead of night to pounce like a bottled-up conscience. It had been waiting for days. As it watched the sun flit over the horizon it realized that time meant little to the hunter, patient for a ripe kill.

Its muscles ached but it maintained its awkward position. It licked saliva from its lips, drooling at the imagined taste of its prey. It did not want to leave a trace of its presence as it squatted on the strongest branch of the tallest tree in the forest.

The shallow-breathed moments lingered in the deep acoustics of the forest. Up here the treeline met the night stars. There was no boundary between present and future, the earthy now and the infinite space of the hereafter above.

On the fifth night it saw its quarry. The boy would pass directly under the boughs as the creature had expected. All it had to do was wait some more.

The boy stopped under the tree. Perhaps he could sense the hunter's pungent bloodlust. The boy looked up at a shadow shifting in the branches, growing bigger, closer. He broke into a run, bolting into dense foliage.

Anger is the most palpable of emotions, scurrying like a damnation rat through an ugly stomach. Try to pull away from it and it will stick to your craw, engulf you. The hunter did not pause to fight the anger. He ran with it. Fury gave him greater speed and he caught up with the boy.

'Boy,' the hunter said in a low growl. The lad stopped, out of breath, cheeks ruddy with exertion. There was nothing but fear in those almond-shaped eyes. 'I only want to talk.'

'I've heard that before,' said the boy as he backed away against a tree trunk. 'What do you want to talk about?' he asked, doubtless playing for time, another few precious seconds of life. Prey always wants to eek out its end before it is eaten, or worse.

'I've been watching you boy,' said the hunter. 'Watching you waste your life. You're worthless. You've achieved nothing. You have no friends, your parents have disowned you, you've never loved anyone, even yourself.'

The boy blushed. How did the hunter know so much about him?

'I can help you,' the hunter continued. 'Money, fame, popularity… so easy to come by. All these treasures are lying around for you to pick up.'

The boy looked down and sure enough there was a sprinkling of gold coins on the forest floor, offering their polished gleam to the starlight. He didn't stoop to pick them up; since when did he take advice from a predator?

'People will continue to tread on you,' the hunter growled, 'use you unless you have power in your village. I ask little in return. A mere boon.'

'And what is that pray tell, dear monster?'

'I want you to share your emotions with me. The elation when you gain your power, your joy and your trepidation, your sexual ecstasies. A small share.'

The boy looked at the hunter's starving eyes and slavering tooth-lined jaws and knew that it would take everything. He declined its offer; better to remain unhappy than have this behemoth following him wherever he went. He shook his head slowly and reached behind the tree trunk. Propped behind the tree was a crudely carved spear. He scooped it in front of him and drove it into the hunter's hide.

The boy had known the creature would be waiting for him and had prepared for it a week beforehand. It had been ensnaring his fellow villagers for some time now, stealing their souls and turning them into unfeeling husks. Now it was dead from a spear wound and he watched as dark blood seeped as heavy as molasses from the wound in its belly.

The boy dragged the creature back to the village and was heralded as a hero. Rewards were heaped upon him and he was given an honored seat on the village council. As he attended year after year of committees, growing fat and complacent, he realized that the hunter had snared him after all.

Over the village hung a moon with a scarred and pockmarked face. It moved slowly, assuredly, knowing that certain events were always destined to be. It would disappear over the vine-green horizon, its cold blue rays no longer tinting the sky. But it would return.

Nick Smith

Aquatic Scenario

See the little fish
Passing time with swim
Dwarfed by brother shoals
Flitting little fin
Not a care at all
Innocent little thing
Floating through the sea
Passing time with swim.

Knows secrets of life
Won't divulge at all
Nobody asks fish
Because he's so small
Speak to fish like him
Do you lots of good
Show you plenty stuff
You never understood.

When caught in a net
Bad fish'man got him
Fish, he don't divulge
Can't pass time with swim
Great secrets of life
Really can't help him
Man don't care for life
He seems rather dim.

Nick Smith

Fish knows he'll be ate
Now he's trapped in net
If you keep secrets
This is what you get.

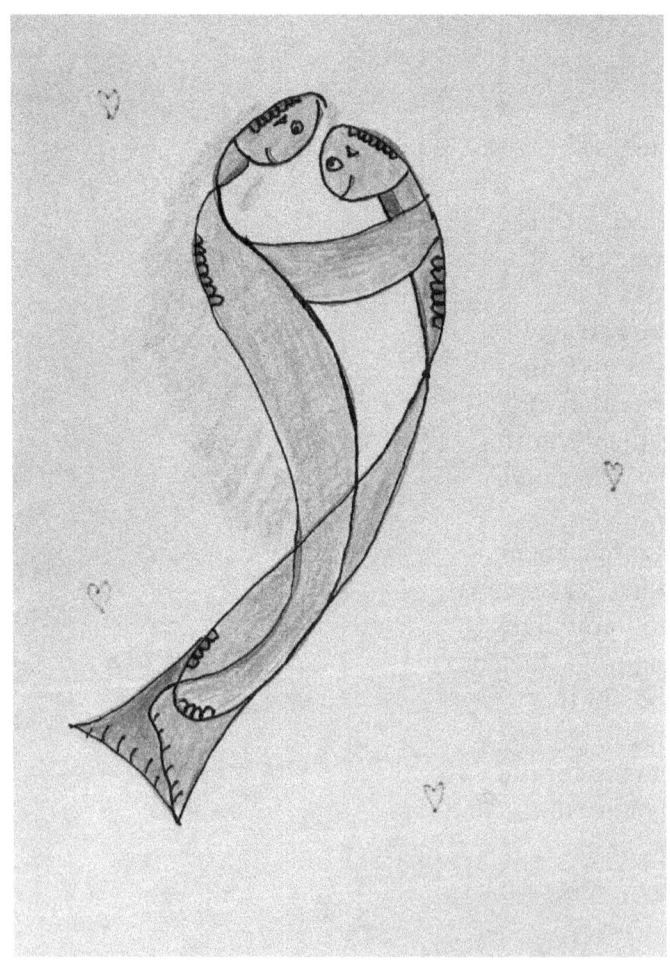

Sharkula Rising

Valentin was cold and tired and lost at sea.

All his loved ones were gone. He'd got used to solitude over the centuries but he'd never felt so alone. The last of his family, with no heirs, no home. The lull of the Atlantic Ocean only added to his sense of isolation. In the darkness of his coffin he didn't know how far he was from land. He knew he would never return to his birthplace.

Valentin had seen the Carpathian Empire topple, the Western empire rise. Feeding on the blood of the young, he'd raised an army of zealots. They had feared and worshiped him. Now they had all faded into time.

Slowly waking, he clutched the earth he lay on. Worms and roaches squirmed in the soil, brought from his homeland. The cool earth helped to give him reassuring sleep.

He sensed that night was approaching, the bloodrush of the moon dragging the tide under the vessel; the quiet of the crew, many of them already slumbering in their cots. Captain Kent up late in his modest cabin, scratching another dull entry in his logbook. The ancient passenger saw all this with his mind's eye but he remained still, waiting for night's pitch to fill the sky.

Captain Kent was a practical man, 30 years at sea, well traveled with a wise mind. He knew the contents of his cargo hold, heard the superstitious mutterings of his crew. He didn't believe his passenger was anything more than a wealthy nocturnal eccentric. He'd visited Eastern Europe, knew that customs were alien there. If his well-paying passenger chose to sleep the days away in the ship's bowels then let him. The sea and the man's purse were important; Kent didn't care if Velentin's mind was as wayward as a storm wind. The captain had handled his ship under many weathers.

Yet he vividly recalled his few encounters with Valentin. On the first night of their journey he'd thought he'd seen Valentin standing on deck – a tall, still figure at the bow, looking out to sea. When the captain had approached, the shadows had parted to reveal nothing but a swirl of sea mist. On most occasions, Valentin never said a word to the captain. Only once had the passenger spoke, respectfully asking that the crew stay away from his low berth. Valentin had a thick Slavic accent, his voice quiet and deep as the ocean floor. The captain had readily agreed, feeling compelled to do so.

Valentin got hungry. He rose from his box and drifted to a large oak trunk. Inside, the remains of a deckhand were unappetizing. The young man was drained of blood; he would have to go overboard. It was time for Valentin to restock his larder.

Beyond the bowels of the freighter, the crew finished its chores for the day. Hans rested at the bow, removed his work gloves, watched the last glimmers of sunset on the open water. He saw a broad fin in the water. The front of the fin was angled backward, the rear jutting straight up. A big shark by the look of it. No matter how beautiful the ocean appeared, it was always deadly.

He fought his fatigue, looked forward to playing poker with his shipmates. He'd lost 20 rubles to Taren in their last game and he was determined to win it back, not because he had anything to spend it on in this Atlantic wasteland but to wipe the smirk off Taren's face.

Hans looked at the sun dipping below the amber-lined meniscus. He felt a cold, salty wind pierce his skin. The sky was dark and cloudless. He turned to the interior lights of the freighter, ready for their comfort. With a start he saw he was not alone. He faced an old man with sad eyes and fine but dirty clothes. The passenger.

'Taking a walk sir?' Hans asked.

Valentin didn't reply. Hans was surprised to see the passenger – he'd started to think the bored crew had made up the mystery man.

'Good night for it,' Hans continued. Valentin took a step closer; Hans couldn't back up. 'Is there anything you need?' the crewman asked.

Hans was a friendly guy, felt he'd overstepped his bounds, was about to turn away but Valentin held his gaze. Stayed silent. Opened his mouth.

Hans saw rows of sharp, jagged teeth, was reminded of the shark he'd seen in the water. He wanted to run, couldn't. His feet felt like they'd taken root to the deck.

Valentin outstretched his arms and gave Hans a thankful embrace. Hans didn't struggle. It was late and he realized how tired he was. That explained why his feet were lead weights. As Valentin sank his teeth into Hans' jugular, the deckhand closed his eyes and slept.

Josef heard a splash. He ran from his post to the bow, shone a light at the water. Ripples and waves. An arm flailing, sinking.

'Man overboard!'

Josef sounded the alarm, threw a life preserver into the water. Hoped he wasn't mistaken, rousing the crewmen for nothing. The darkness played tricks on the most seasoned of sailors but it was better to be safe.

Matthew had a big stake in the game. He trusted his instincts, appreciated his run of good luck. His friend owed him money they hadn't even earned yet. The only player that posed a threat to him, Walenksi, hadn't joined the table. This was Matthew's night.

Matthew dealt a fresh hand. His luck was holding up. Until he heard Josef's yell, his friends jumped up, the pot scattered.

'Man overboard!'

Really? In these deep waters they'd be lucky to find a whale.

Matthew followed his crewmates onto the deck, saw Josef leaning over the rail looking frantic.

'Who the hell is it?' Matthew asked. 'Who's damn fool enough to fall in the drink?'

A swift head count showed one man missing. Josef wasn't imagining things after all.

'Hans was supposed to come play cards with us,' said Matthew. 'Never turned up.'

'Because he went for a looong swim.'

The freighter turned about, retracing its wake in search of Hans. The crewmen shone lights into the water but there was no sign of their friend.

'Shark got him,' said Josef sadly.

'You could be right,' said Matthew. 'That boy's fishfood right enough.'

The freighter righted its course, the captain already planning a letter to Hans' parents. A search was conducted from bow to stern just to make sure Hans hadn't collapsed drunk in a corner somewhere. He could not be found; neither was the passenger Valentin.

Within a few hours the men were in their berths, lights out, ship rocking a little on the water. Everyone but Hans was present and correct, Josef could tell as he panned his flashlight round the sleeping quarters careful not to shine the beam in anyone's face.

Something was wrong, though. An unsettling silence. There was no snoring, deep breathing or coughing. Dead quiet.

Josef moved closer to the nearest birth where Higgins lay. He was asleep. He *had* to be asleep. Josef held his hand in front of Higgins' gawp-open mouth, felt no breath. Used the edge of the flashlight beam to look closer.

'What the hell?'

Two puncture wounds marked Higgins' pale throat. Dark red blood trickled along his collarbone. An animal bite, or –

Higgins' eyes snapped open.

Josef fell back, fumbling his flashlight. He held it up to defend himself but the other men had left their beds, surrounding him.

'Do not drain him completely,' said Valentin, appearing from the shadows. 'Leave a little in his veins for later.'

Josef screamed, engulfed by the possessed crew. Higgins lunged at his throat but was rocked off-balance – the freighter had hit rough water.

Josef pulled away, the men following him onto the rain-spattered deck. High, rolling waves beckoned ahead. He heard Valentin say, 'let him run, he has nowhere to go,' and he made for a lifeboat, hoping Higgins and the others would not follow him.

They followed him. He grasped the lifeboat release as the vessel hawed crazily, making his stomach lurch. He could jump into the water away from these fiends but he didn't fancy his chances in the waves below.

'Get off my ship.' The Captain had not been afflicted by Valentin's curse; holed up in his cabin, he'd been trying to plot a course around the storm. Too late now. He stood on the deck, facing the pale passenger.

'This vessel belongs to me now,' Valentin snarled. 'The crew are mine. The ship is mine.'

A monstrous wave crashed against the hull. The captain leveled a flare gun at Valentin. 'I told you -'

Valentin's form dispersed into mist and reformed around the captain, smothering him in darkness. The captain fell to the deck, an unconscious, bloody husk.

Josef made the most of this unholy distraction. With a clunk, the lifeboat was ready to go. Higgins and the rest of the undead mob were still unsettled by the night storm. Josef leaped into the boat, snatched mid-jump by Valentin who sank a taloned hand into Josef's arm. Valentin's sharp ancient nails dug deep and Josef had to tug hard to free himself. Josef fell back onto the ship, crowded by the crew; Valentin fell into the water far below.

With the crew lost to reason, the freighter was flooded, slowly sinking. Valentin sank as well, into the Gulf of Mexico, away from the rising sunlight. As his surroundings darkened his strength increased. He could still taste the captain's blood in his mouth, saw the man's mauled body float nearby. More blood flowed from it, attracting an underwater predator that Valentin had heard of but never encountered before.

A Great White swam toward the body, more curious than hungry. It was a true sea beast, over ten feet long, face ugly with scars, sinking rows of razor teeth into the captain and tearing off a juicy arm. Though Valentin let the currents take him away from the feast, the shark soon turned to him with its mouth opened wide.

Valentin stopped trying to flee. He struck out at the shark, digging his deadly talons into cartilage, biting a chunk from the shark's flank. The shark snapped back, nipping at a slice of Valentin's thigh. The count kicked away from the fierce predator, watching as the sinking freighter sucked the shark away from him. Faint, lungs full of water, Valentin drifted down into the dark.

Though the freighter was lost to men, the creatures of the deep soon made it their home. Shoals of tiny fish used it as a shelter; larger ones hid from their hunters in open cabins and the sunken mess hall.

Lord of this wreck was a Great White with eyes more ghoulish than any of its brethren, teeth sharper, hunger greater. The shark avoided sunlight and the crossbar of the ship's mast. It would guard the old vessel for many days to come.

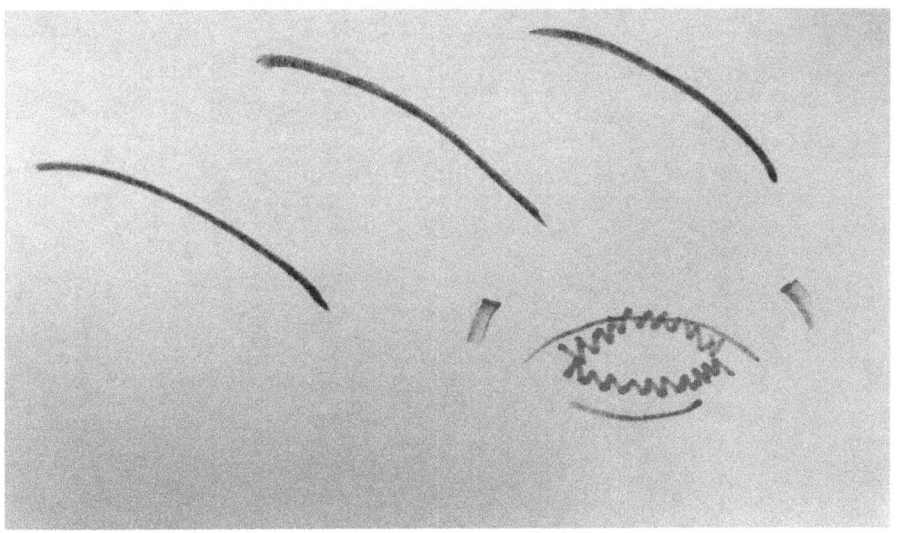

Nick Smith

Untitled

On a rainbow colored cloud-stopped day
The deck beckons
An oasis of quiet dewdrop kisses
Looking out on a scrabbled back lawn
Where a bow-tied owl wind spinner perches,
Facing the gate now, shy from our canoodling.

A string of lights grins across the back fence
Giving the grass a cosseting glow
Two Adirondack chairs sit far from the bee's nest
Close to the droning AC unit

My chair purple, yours green
Matching our ResortQuest branded sunglasses.
When the seats are wet we stare at them
Judging whether to sit down and face damp consequences
Or pace the deck like land-locked sea captains.

Clouds poke sneer-smeared faces at an amorous couple in faded robes
Squirrels perform their high-wire act on the fence
Striking Washington post poses
Daring us to watch them dance.

They're too limber to be glimpsed for long,
Scooting up palm fronds, rustling their presence.
We don't want them to move fast.
We need time to slow down, the leftover sun to linger on our legs,
The rain's needle drops to hit their brakes,
Squirrels playing musical statues
Bee's buzz turning to a honeying hum

Nick Smith

The owl spinning slow as a 78
The patch grass resting from its weedy growth
So our kisses last.

Quiche Not for Lorraine

An Eat Happy recipe

INGREDIENTS

11/2 cups of All Purpose Flour
3/4 tsp. of salt
½ chilled cup of shortening
4 tbsp. of very cold water
4 eggs
2 cups of grated cheese
1 cup of half-and-half
1 tbsp. of butter
1 ½ cups of bacon, torn to pieces as if by a hungry goat

INSTRUCTIONS

Pour flour in bowl and stir – no clumping!
Add ½ tsp. of salt
Add shortening
Stir, but not so much that shortening can't be seen
Trickle one tbs. of water onto one quarter of the flour and mix into that quarter
Slowly add the other 3 tbs. of water in the same manner, one quarter of the bowl at a time.
Flatten into a circle. Cover with Saran wrap for 30 minutes or (if you're not too hungry) longer
Once cooled, flatten the dough some more with a roller until the circle can cover a 9" dish
Layer the dough on the pie dish, trimming excess on the rim

Nick Smith

Cover and refrigerate for another 30 minutes
Get your oven ready, don't head out on the highway - 375° please
Fry bacon
Scramble eggs, adding the cheese and half-and-half
Add the broken-up bacon to the eggs
Pour the mixture onto the piecrust
Cook for 45 minutes approximately – the bacon should look well
cooked and the cheese bubbly
Allow to cool a little
It's ready to eat happy!

December Duet

Far from passion, pain and guilt
In caverns far from inn or church
Their kind in coldness ever dwell
With folded wings they take the hanged man's perch.

Dead men's spirits in the air
Blind to the fate that nature gave
We envy their winged escape
Yet share their destined grave.

So high yet seeing naught but dark
Our souls with burdens great
Leathered limbs caress the sky
Gods blinded by the weight.

The wheel turns, the spirit memories remain
A never-changing face
More sooted than the world below
Too numb to change their place.

Nick Smith

Bare Legs

Bare legs

White as cottage cheese

Reveal themselves

Nick Smith

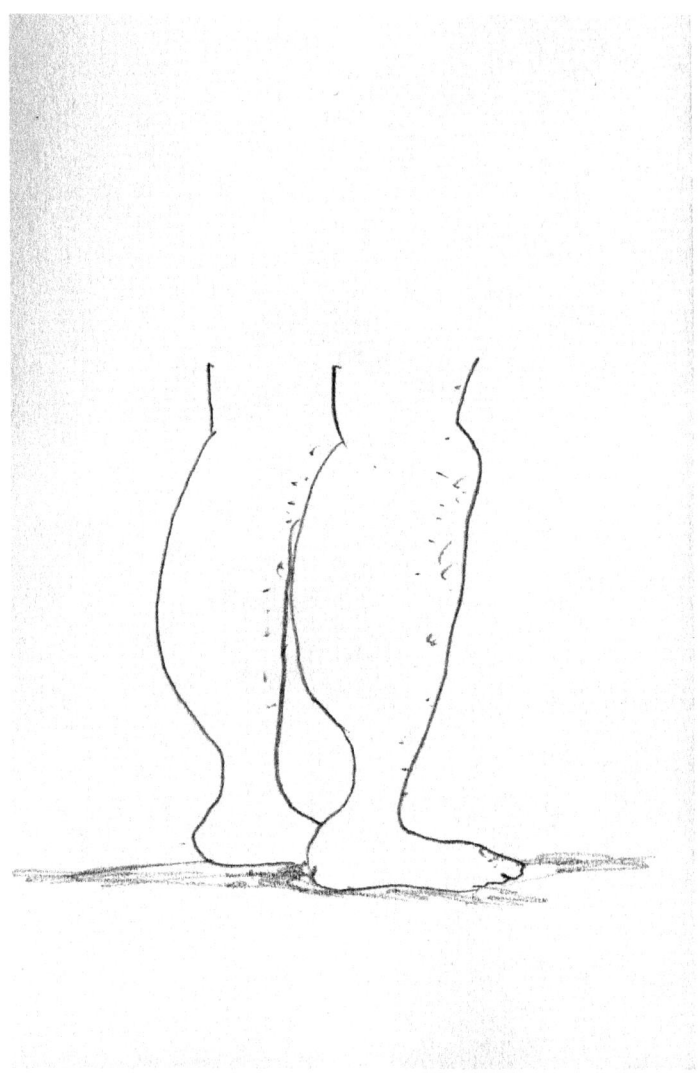

Sweet, Sweet Tablet
An Eat Happy dessert

INGREDIENTS

1kg Caster sugar
125g Unsalted butter (+ as required to grease the pan)
350ml Condensed milk
1/2tsp of salt
250ml whole milk
1/2tsp vanilla extract

INSTRUCTIONS

Pour sugar and whole milk into a large saucepan
Add butter and salt
Pour in condensed milk
Heat on medium high
Bring to boil
Stir occasionally
Add vanilla; stir constantly until mixture is thick
Spread on a baking tray, let cool for an hour
Break off a piece and enjoy the Scottish sugar rush!

Nick Smith

Slow Down or Fall Down

It took us two years to get to Charleston, South Carolina. We sold our cottage in Bonnybridge, a tiny Scottish village, only to learn that it would take many months of paperwork and medical tests before we'd be considered as immigrants to the US. The process was extra strict after 9/11 and we didn't have an exact timeline for our trip so we rented a titchy house not far from Sherwood Forest in England and waited.

My Scottish wife Ros had already been asked to work as a nurse at the Medical University of South Carolina (MUSC) hospital in downtown Charleston. In return for eighteen months' indentured service (as she called it), she would earn a green card for herself and her family.

Just when we thought we'd be stuck in limbo forever, we got the go-ahead to fly to the States. We left our land of cold weather, warm beer and petty bureaucracy for a new world of warm weather, cold beer and petty bureaucracy. The move would be a huge culture shock for me, though I didn't know it at the time. Luckily we had a guide to help ease us into our new American life – a good ol' guy called Georgia Jim.

As our plane prepared to land and we caught our first glimpse of Charleston, we remarked on its color. The land below was green and sunny, even though we were only seeing a strip of highway. We would have found the sight welcoming but we were distracted by our three-year-old son Sam, who had started to cry.

We couldn't blame him. He'd sat patiently through an eight-hour flight from London, England to Newark, mesmerized by the in-flight movies. He'd waited in line as we worked our way through Immigration, Ros tearfully hugging the official who stamped her passport. Now Sam had to endure another, shorter flight to Charleston Airport that wasn't equipped with that all-important in-flight

93

entertainment, and he was letting his fellow passengers know that he was bored.

We'd brought plenty of toys to entertain him. Determined to travel light, we'd only brought our cat Tips and three suitcases with us. Apart from a few clothes, they were filled with Sam's gear, including his bicycle. I'd dismantled his beloved red bike and squeezed it into one of the cases. We kept the bike for years until I gave up trying to put it back together and bought him a new one.

Jetlag quietened Sam as we left the plane and collected our bags in the airport. We were greeted by Jim, a Harley-riding 'Nam vet from Savannah, Georgia who'd been hired by Ros' sponsor company to welcome us and help us get oriented in our first week in Charleston. He took an immediate shine to Sam, who hid behind me to shelter from Jim's hearty greetings.

Georgia Jim had a chocolate brown GM van with a 'for sale' sign on the window. The notice went on to tell potential buyers, '87, runs good, smokes some.' There was plenty of room for us in the van and we rattled over to our rented apartment in West Ashley, Jim's stereo leaking smooth jazz.

'Mebbe in the morning I could take y'all to Krispy Kreme,' said Jim, his mouth rounding into a doughnut hole shape. 'When their sign's on, you just pop one o' them doughnuts in your mouth and they melt.' Jim was a big fan of the franchise, his heart glowing in sync with that sign.

Within a whirlwind few days we'd figured out how to use a coffee maker, eaten shrimp 'n' grits, got hooked on pecan pie and admired the cranes that flew overhead on Folly Beach. Jim would wear his darkest sunglasses explaining that, 'the ladies can't see me looking at 'em, though they can see what I'm thinkin.' He would berate the kids bellyboarding in the shallows, shouting: 'You need water to do that on, boy.'

Georgia Jim got a big kick out of his role as our mentor but he always kept his cool, even when Sam's toenail got jammed with a splinter and the boy started howling. We were trying to buy a used car at the time; Sam's cries became so heartbreaking that I bought the first Toyota on the lot from an Honest John salesman.

Jim even kept his cool when he joined me for a test drive. I wasn't feeling cool at all – I was driving an automatic for the first time, on a different side of the car, on a different side of the road. 'You're scaring the other drivers,' Jim told me as I pulled out of the lot. 'An' you're scaring me. Step on the gas, you're gonna get run over...' meaning I'd get rammed if I didn't keep my speed up. I learned the hard way that my fellow motorists were like desperate single men. They didn't take time to give the right signals when they made a pass.

For Jim, a car was only as good as its AC. If it was ice cold as soon as it was turned on, he was happy. No wonder – we'd arrived in mid-July, lapping up the salty heat, and apparently the humidity slowed Charlestonians down some.

When I found a gas station and topped up my tank, Jim asked me to get a couple of sodas from the kiosk. I started to run over to it but my guide called after me, 'no! You gotta walk. Nobody runs here.' I like to run – it's one of my few ways of keeping fit – but I figured that Jim meant I'd scare the gas attendant if I charged straight for him, so I slowed down. I didn't realize until later that I'd have to reduce my pace and stop rushing around to avoid dehydrating – slow down or fall down – and that's a great excuse to take things easy.

Buying the car opened a bewildering floodgate of tax forms, insurance quotes and visits to the DMV. But no matter what red-taped hoops we had to jump through, the sun always shone. If you've ever seen a Scottish family on vacation, you might have noticed that they get all wild and noisy when they find an outdoor swimming pool. Now imagine living somewhere that's too cold and rainy to entertain the idea of such a pool. Wouldn't you go wild too?

We slowly thawed out after living through a particularly sickly, snowy British spring; we were tourists who never had to go home. This was our honeymoon period, filled with sunbathing, free time to spend with our son, and shopping for fancy goods for our apartment. That gave me time to start acclimatizing.

I was in a daze, losing my wallet and keys, stepping in nests of feisty fire ants, falling afoul of traffic cops. Back home I knew how everything worked, here I was a fish out of water across the pond and up a creek. A song kept playing on the radio – Jason Mraz's *The Remedy* – reminding me not to worry my life away, his music soothing my hopscotch pulse as I navigated South Carolina's potholed highways. But unfortunately Georgia Jim was there to help me less and less as he helped other immigrants find their feet. After a week, he left us to fend for ourselves.

By August the honeymoon had ended. We knuckled down to work and Sam chose a daycare center on that criterion most important to toddlers – it had a cool schoolyard. We hadn't known Jim for very long but his effect on us was profound; we shopped and ate at the same places he introduced us to for many years to come. The displays of generosity that we constantly experienced in Charleston mirrored Jim's munificence. Those hints he gave us of what it meant to be American informed us as we became citizens ourselves. They remind us how essential first impressions can be, lighting beacons in the mire of our memories.

Nick Smith

Will Power

If you pay for my obituary in the Northwest Florida Daily News,
I don't want any of the religious razzmatazz.

I am not transitioning to a heavenly home.
I have not been called away like a dog who's played too long in the doggie park.
I've died in an awkwardly flabby privileged bedroom pose in the middle of the night.
I'm dead and I can't take my Game of Thrones DVDs with me.

I don't want my academic achievements listed
Followed by my stunted career highs
(Director of IT, RIP)
although I would like a mention of the time I worked as a bodyguard
for the school rich kid when I was 12 and earned 50p
And I'd also like it on record that *I* should have got the High School
Magazine Award for Best Editor, not Mark Moore.
Heck, I even stood up when they announced the prize then had to sit
back down again when they didn't say my name.

It should have been me, I worked like a slave on that damn thing,
that's all I'm saying.

My soul will not be kind and loving
It'll be pissed. It had soul plans.
No one will have fond cherished memories of me
Because I don't like them much either.

Nick Smith

I will not pass away after a brief illness
I will cry like a butt-ugly baby and take as long as Sean Connery takes
to die in *The Untouchables*.

My funeral will happen at an inconvenient time,
Like the middle of the night,
So people have to get out of bed and drag their warm, living asses to
my cold dark resting place.

I will not be buried and invisible
But burned and ground into worms of powdered ink so that readers can
read me
In the middle of the night.

So Totally Delicious
An Eat Happy dessert

INGREDIENTS

1 12 oz. package of La Choy chow mein noodles
1 12 oz. bag of butterscotch chips
1 16 oz. can of cocktail peanuts
2 tbsp. of butter

INSTRUCTIONS

Melt butterscotch chips with a little butter in a double boiler
MAKE SURE NO STEAM GETS IN (no clumping)
Make sure water is at a low simmer
Stir while cooking until butterscotch is melted
Remove from double boiler
Add equal parts nuts 'n' noodles
Add the butter
Stir until well coated
Drop a little heap on a baking tray lined with wax paper, repeat, allow
to set (takes approximately 30 minutes in a fridge)
Enjoy the deliciousness

Nick Smith

Godburger

Doug stood on his tiptoes, trying to see over the crowd. Rollo was in the thick of the action, standing in the brand new megabranch of his fast food chain, a carnival barking mad purveyor of greasy meat. Rollo was Doug's hero.

Rollo was the Burgermeister, the ribbon cutting figurehead of the Eat Happy Corporation, a beefy Colonel Sanders, salesperson extraordinaire, singer of earworm jingles.

I like burgers
I eat them whenever I want
I will
Until the cows come home

Doug held Kate's hand tight, listening closely as Rollo addressed his audience.

'In here we've got meat. None of that other rubbish that gets stuffed in burgers to make them look bigger – no lettuce, no cucumber and *especially*,' Rollo squashed up his face with disgust, 'no pickles – nothing good for you whatsoever.'

Men and women, boys and girls lined up for their food. Their stomachs rumbled a harmonious tune, their feet shuffled in time toward the register. But the busy trade didn't slow Rollo's spiel.

'Even the buns are unhealthy as we can possible make them, loaded with carbs and gluten. I'm sure you'll agree it's the least nutritious food that tastes the best and I reckon if you want to be healthy get down to the gym, not here. Our buns have got plenty of salt and the least amount of genuine bread possible. Our burgers're mostly meat because that's what the customers want. And the customer's always right.'

Nick Smith

Doug expected to see some of his friends at the big opening of the new Eat Happy but he couldn't make out any of the red blazers or grey sweaters of their school uniforms. There were plenty of kids, some skinny as snakes, some fat as footballs but none that he recognized or wanted to befriend. Men and women pushed past him in their fight to get fed – accountants with their briefcases held flat like trays, sad housewives brandishing their shopping money, builders ready to fill their bulging guts and teachers bossing the other customers into an orderly line.

These people had been content to wait hours for the restaurant to open and paid for the overpriced food without complaint. They didn't smile or chat amongst themselves, looking at the $10 meals advertised above the counter and drooling at the pictures of *bas cuisine* wrapped in golden breadcrumbs.

Thanks to his well-connected parents, Doug had Rollo's ear and that meant no line and no wait for Doug and Kate's food. They both got tasty Eat Meals in tasteless green bags. All they had to do in return was let Rollo gas on about how great his burgers were. Doug didn't mind humoring the eccentric man; he couldn't wait to tell his school friends about the meeting, whether they believed him or not.

Behind the scenes, away from the chiming kitchen and munching customers, was the pumping heart of the megabranch – a machine bristling with pistons, grinders, terabytes of deli data and tenderizing tentacles.

The machine was huge. Bigger than Doug could have imagined – bigger than that. It tottered ten times over Doug's head, casting a shadow across to the door. The computer that controlled it was as big as a tank. Sitting at the keyboard, controlling the machine's very pop and spark, Rollo hammered instructions into his creation.

'Big enough, innit?' said Rollo without looking up. 'Know what this is for, boy?'

Doug shook his head although he had a good idea. On top of the machine were bulldog teeth, chewing on something with a gasoline chaser. Clawed arms stretched out on either side of its square middle, scooping up anything that came within their grasp. Doug retreated toward the door, looking for his companion.

'Where's Kate?'

'I asked you a question,' Rollo snapped. 'Since you seem unwilling to answer, I guess I'll have to give you a demonstration of what my machine can do,' he pressed a button on his keyboard, 'and why my Eat Happy chain is so all-fired popular.'

'Time to add the secret ingredient Kate.' Rollo keyed a new command into the computer. An overhead chute opened up, unleashing ooze into the machine.

'Know what slime molds are?' Kate asked. She was by the door – Doug's only means of escape – locking it tight. 'They're little creatures, living fungi that live in forests. They'll eat anything in their path, digest it, make themselves bigger. They're unstoppable.'

Rollo closed the chute as two last drips of goo fell into the toothsome trough. He dusted his palms together, a job well done, and cocked an ear to listen to the sucking sounds of the slime.

'I spent three years in the forests,' Rollo bragged, 'capturing slime molds, breeding them to produce huge supermolds. They're my pets.'

'Must be hard for a guy like you to make friends,' said Doug, trying to sound brave.

'I only had a little burger bar back then,' said Rollo. 'Earned my keep flipping meat on a roadside griddle. But I found out a funny thing. One of my pets escaped from their glass tank, got merged with a burger. You know that was the tastiest bite anyone had ever taken? I was an overnight sensation. People came from all over the place to try my food. I never shared my recipe with anyone – until Kate came along.'

'What's so special about her?' asked Doug, annoyed that a girl had fooled him into trusting her so easily.

'As soon as I clapped eyes on her I knew she was important, Doug.' Rollo smiled. One of his teeth was pitch as night. 'She was bad through and through. No one would ever suspect a sweet-looking girl of kicking cats, spitting in her mother's soup or spraying graffiti on the walls at school. But all these things are child's play to Kate. She was the one who discovered the other important ingredient in my burgers – the one that has folks coming back for more and more.'

A shiver chilled Doug's spine. 'Why is that then?' he asked.

'That would be telling.'

Doug realized that Kate had backed him up against the ladder. 'You want me to climb up there?' He pointed at the machine mouth.

'Don't be silly. Only a complete fool would go up that ladder with all that slime in there.'

A complete fool? Doug thought of the lines of people at the counter, hungry for their fast food. He looked at Kate, the Charlie of this ghoulish factory, and realized what the second secret ingredient was.

'I'll blow the whistle,' said Doug, not sounding very convincing. Rollo shook his head and pointed at the ladder. Overwhelmed, Doug began to climb. *Never meet your heroes,* he told himself. They might feed you to a burger monster.

He still clutched his Eat Happy Meal in his hand. He'd lost his appetite. Tossed the bright green paper bag into the central grinder like garbage in a can.

'No!' Rollo yelled, reaching up at the machine. Sliding down the ladder, Doug grabbed Kate's meal and slam-dunked that into the machine mouth too. The burger monster growled, trying to digest processed supermold, getting eaten from within.

'What have you done child?' Rollo cried. The machine's tentacles lashed out, grabbed Rollo and Kate and dragged them into its bowels. Doug forced the door open, taking on last glance back to see the machine pop at the seams in a frenzy of gushing fat.

'Eat me,' said Doug, slamming the door and walking confidently out of the megabranch, staff and customers staring at him, wondering what had caused all the noise and screams.

Doug kept walking. He had a lot of work to do, many machines to shut down before fast food junkies could eat happily ever after.

The Magical Properties Of Letters

Thea lay on her back, aching and dizzy. She didn't know where she was. In her long-ago, distant childhood she'd been guided, taught, by a select few people. Many of her mannerisms, the way she nodded her head when happy, they way she talked had come from somewhere. But the names and faces of her teachers escaped her, as did the reason why she had been locked in a white room.

Someone had pushed her in, picked from the crowd of Saturday shoppers. Thea wasn't sure who. She had felt something shove her into the white, flinched at cold breath on the back of her neck. Nothing beyond these sensations.

The room reminded her of job interviews, clinics, the school gym. In none of these places had she felt so vulnerable. There were no windows, and Thea could not see the door through which she'd entered. Yet someone was watching her – maybe a few people – and willing her to react in some way.

So Thea reacted. She sat down cross-legged and sulked, closing her eyes to shut out the brilliant white. She heard a voice, a chorus of voices, hiss in her ear.

Theifofbutnd/woodland tales/small word, big world/river swathes off

Thea opened damp eyes. Nothing there. The sounds had been as imaginary as they had seemed solid. She stared at the opposite wall looking for cracks, jambs, door hinges. For the first time she noticed that the walls had a common grain, a patterned, circular groove that ran around the room. She shuffled to one side on her knees, reaching out to touch a wall. It seemed to retreat before her fingers, then yielded to her, dry and hungry.

Nick Smith

Memories struck like arrowheads – a game of tennis, a lonely child, a military life. She didn't know whether the life was hers or not. Though distant, the recollections were strong – infrequent, heavy-scented, mingling with the voices.

River swathes off toward the horizon, besieged by grey mud banks/converted warehouses spill their guts with waves, signs painted on the gables/such a character/the Louisiana, a pub disguised as a steamboat, stands

She had known some attractive men in her time. She'd done all the chasing, they'd plumped her and plied her and used her. A blur of faces and tongues and egos. Their names were irrelevant. She'd enjoyed teasing them, her tennis skirt skiffing about her thighs. The best men, the prize catches, the captains and majors, had seen through her.

On the corner of Bleeth Street/The Bank of Scotland's revolving doors wait for kids to use them as a playground pawn/they open with a wish. I'm surprised by the tellers' accents/I didn't know there that many Scots in

Thea had a goal: to get out of the room, get home. She couldn't recall ever having such a strong sense of purpose. She hammered at the walls, slapping ineffectual fists in the hope that someone would hear. There was no hollow sound of a doorway no matter where she tried, and the room seemed to absorb her blows – there were no echoes, no paint cracks, only the muffled thud of her hands. When they began to redden she stopped. Someone would turn up to release her, or gloat, or worse.

This was an experiment. That was it. An endurance test to examine Thea's response to sudden isolation. That would explain her sense that she was being studied, though there was no sign of a microphone or camera lens. She'd be let out soon, told it was all a joke, given a fat cheque to keep quiet. All she had to do was wait, control her breathing, remain calm. There was no way she'd put on a show for some voyeuristic boffin.

She closed her eyes, let her shoulders sag. Still couldn't remember much about herself. She'd been drugged, given something by her captors that had affected her mind. The amnesia couldn't be permanent – jigsaw piece flashes of memory were already appearing with increased regularity – but the theory would explain her confusion and paranoia. The memories of sex and death were disconcerting and the voices in her head scared her. Curiosity kept her sane.

She had been a WAAC in the last world war, bright, athletic, with a high libido. Thea had always spoken her mind, expressing unpopular opinions. She had been as beautiful as she was inquisitive. Blotting paper soaking up all the information around her. She had wanted to know everybody's secrets.

Closing her eyes helped. The memories started to piece together, painstaking, rewarding when they formed a recognisable image. The WAAC girl had owned a flat in Chelmsford, six pairs of shoes, a cat called Bing and a rusty bicycle. She had been a white witch.

Thea Vevey, giggler, dreamer, self-styled expert on the magical properties of numbers and letters. Their cold curls held an enormous fascination for her – the letter E, with its ellipse: a symbolic demonstration of the transcendent unity that pervaded all duality. A and O, the alpha and omega that embraced creation. The L with its righteous right angle; the X, negative in form, strong in its spiritual origins.

She'd scared some boys off with her hobby; used her spells to woo them back. Her great love – her great love Harry had been ensnared with a novice ritual. She'd slaughtered a lamb to get her way – what greater indication of her love could there have been?

Names that begin with S are the names for snakes/initial applications for deferment of payment for Class 2 and Class 4/Certainly has no

Nick Smith

regrets   about   being   part   of   Hollywood's   most   important
franchises/together   with   more   information   about   deferment   and
refunds/long   been   cited   by   rock   critics   as   an   outstanding   example   of
his unique lead vocals

A candlelit dinner of pork chops and powdered egg. Love rationed with the weekly messages. Masks worn by everyone, air raid or no air raid. Curses placed on unkind colleagues, and hexes on Hitler. Her best beloved had discarded her of course, traded her in for some plain as pudding seamstress with longer hair and a lower drive, and the split had hit Thea hard. She'd been so angry back then, frustrated in her poverty, bad luck, her cramped home. She'd survived, shut herself away from her man friends and family, closeted with her spells. Determined to wait until the bombs stopped falling, she'd stayed locked away for longer.

When she'd stepped out of her flat twenty years later, she had been more powerful, more thoughtful, her eyes a little less bright. Determined to use her dubious skills in white magic for a greater purpose than chasing men, she had set up a small health food store and peddled herbs, salads and vegetarian cook books. Before her time she would have added, as she'd been ready to catch the health food fad.

Queen Thea, rich businesswoman Thea, sometimes she'd used her way with witchery to heal people with minor ailments who visited her establishment, but restricted her cookery to the books. No frog legs or bats' eyes for this old girl. Her determined vows not to meddle had lasted until she had seen Captain George, a retired naval hero, whose lantern jaw and flambeau eyes had struck her in one glance.

How to catch a man: In a box room at the back of the store, take a pile of books (various authors) and a large pair of scissors. Wallpaper scissors are best here, but make sure they're very sharp before beginning.

With as much frenzy and delirium as is possible to muster, tear pages from the books and scatter them around the room. Take random leaves and carve them into tiny bits with the scissors. Take a deep breath then clear away the bindings, dust jackets and spines, leaving the pieces of paper piled up in the middle of the floor. Dispose of the rest of the books in a trashcan fire on the back lawn. Push the remaining pieces of paper together so that they form pages. Don't worry if they don't make sense; the more whisked-up they are the better.

I want that man/where has he gone/where did he go?/I need him/I need to get out of here/get out of hell free

Thea blinked and the walls appeared to flicker, lose their solidity. She rubbed her eyes and stared around the room again, disorientated by the blank surroundings. No landmarks, no sense of space or distance. Her experimenters were obviously cold and cruel, and her patience was wearing thin.

With a burst of pent-up energy she ran and threw herself at the opposite wall. Scrabbling upwards with her hands clawed, she began to climb. The surface that had seemed too sheer at first managed to support her fingers and toes as she pulled herself up towards the ceiling. Looking up, she decided that she had nowhere else to go. Perhaps the opaque tent above her head wasn't as solid as the floor had been.

Thea had never been scared of heights. She knew what human beings were capable of; people frightened her, not invisible abstractions like gravity. However, her disorientation increased as she climbed, and the wall that had seemed ten feet high stretched upwards towards the cold-colored canopy, perpetually beyond arm's reach.

Old man's whisker/grinding someone's bark to make my bread/she decided she had amnesia when she couldn't remember her English teacher's name/forget me not/Bob Marley room/who's that knockin'/Just for a change let's escape all those movies/fox glove/homes giving shelter cast the longest shadows/she was just a character/stuff that matters

Nick Smith

The cut-and-paste pages had formed spells of probability, the sheer randomness of the words making a magic more powerful than any sorcerer's elixir. Thea had sat cross-legged, blocking her womb from the world, with the scattered paper before her. She had read slowly, carefully, making sure that she enunciated every syllable in a precise manner. It had taken her four hours to read the sacred sheaf, and she had been pleased as punch when she'd finished. Laying back, arching her stiff spine, Thea had closed her eyes for a second and woken up –

In the white room, Thea kept climbing. Despite her lofty perch she still maintained her grip. The wall molded itself to her fingers, helped support her, stopped her from falling to her death. Feet pressed against the grey grooves, pushing her towards the ceiling.

Grey grooves. It was a question of point of view, the way you looked at things. From a certain angle she could see the grey formed curlicues, tails, long vertical lines that she had missed before. Funny. Very faint, but still funny. When she's woken up, from her disadvantage point on the ground, the walls had looked perfectly white. Too perfect.

Now the floor was a pearl pool far beneath and there was no way that Thea could turn back. If she couldn't find a way out, then at least she could escape the gaze of those imagined men in white coats beyond the padded cell.

Reaching up, searching for another handhold, Thea touched the ceiling and her shoulders tensed. The ceiling didn't budge, as unforgiving as the rest of her life. The climb had been a waste of time. There was no escape hatch, no bright skylight and she was still being watched. She was sure of it. If anything the voices in her head had grown louder as she ascended.

Halfway house life/you left them camping there/in Summertime, the bed dries up/more interested in your own hedonistic half-life/there's a war to win on the nose, you know

No one was going to let her out of her cell. No gold-lit door was going to open, Dale Winton standing there, 'you've won Superparanoia Sweep and here's your prize, goodbye Missus, there's the exit – turn to the right for the way out.' She was trapped forever, clinging by her fingertips to the padded dungeon from hell. She still had no inkling if how she'd got there; perhaps the izzy whizzy spells had something to do with it, but she'd never been one to make assumptions (learned that from Mum, don't take sweets from strangers, don't open more than two bank accounts at the same time, don't presume to assume anything).

A vomitous lurch, a sensation of almost falling… she had leaned too far backwards, complacent. She didn't want to die. It would hurt too much and she hadn't done all the things she wanted with her life – scuba diving, parachute jumping, the usual stunts. Thea took a couple of heaving deep breaths, wished she'd brought her climbing boots, counted to fourteen to fight her panic (another trick her mother had taught her).

Look down, she told herself, *look down, sod what they tell you on TV. It's not going to hurt,* and the grey marks she'd glanced at earlier begged a second glance. The black lines that traversed the grey and white were bolder, braver from this viewpoint. One line towered past her nose, a thick tree-long line, bookended by two short horizontal strokes. Like a life-size letter I. The other shadows and pits in the wall had calligraphic elements, and she began to see other letters. Like a magic eye graph, the truth appeared before her. The walls were lined with thin, hollow, look-at-them-straight-on-angled-and-you-won't-see-them-at-all letters. Thea peered down and saw –

Letters. Sentences, paragraphs… a world's worth of words as plain as the head on her shoulders. She'd had to climb this high, take herself so far away from the ground to see it. The words looked familiar. Like a character trapped in a story, she could see her experience read before her eyes. The black lettering sandal-strapped the walls in close high curls, overwhelming her, making her lose her grip.

Nick Smith

She tried to grab the tail of a y on her way down but it slanted too much for her to grab. The words were spell-ridden, words with which her story had been written. The grey swirls were cold watermarks, floating past her as she fell.

```
                                              T
                                        H
                                            E
                                                       A


                                        V
                                          E
                                          V
                                          E
                                        Y
```

Funny, that sensation of falling. First you think you're swimming, expecting the water to support your back. Then you find there's no support at all. That's when you drop.

Don't disappoint the readers/voyeurs, the morbid bleeders/her memories so select, given to her by her creator

She didn't just drop. She plummeted downwards, a fat block boulder –
       Thea lay on her back, aching and dizzy. She didn't know where she was. In her long-ago, distant childhood she'd been guided, taught, by a select few people. Many of her mannerisms, the way she nodded her head when happy, they way she talked had come from somewhere. But the names and faces of her teachers escaped her, as did the reason why she had been locked in a white room.

Eat Happy

Nick Smith

The Nighttime Traveler's Tale

I listen when it's quiet
Admiring the calm the stillness
Broken by your tender breathing
Lying night-naked with you
Under the blue haven of our comforter
Your soft hair haloed by a string of owl lights on
                                 the wall.

I cry when it's silent
Grateful for your kindly touch
Waiting for the next fingertip stroke
That tells me I'm worth touching
Watching for moonlight window slivers
Marking their passage across my body.

I listen when it's noiseless
Admiring your sleep-scent
Holding you tight when you desire it
In your Darcy-girl dreams
I drift off, join you
Seek you in your tranquil nighttime world.

www.ingramcontent.com/pod-product-compliance
Lightning Source LLC
Chambersburg PA
CBHW071132250626

47159CB00006B/2216